Agatha

Girl of Mystery

GROSSET & DUNLAP
Published by the Penguin Group
Penguin Group (USA) Inc., 375 Hudson Street, New York, New York 10014, USA
Penguin Group (Canada), 90 Eglinton Avenue East, Suite 700, Toronto, Ontario M4P 2Y3, Canada
(a division of Pearson Penguin Canada Inc.)
Penguin Books Ltd, 80 Strand, London WC2R 0RL, England
Penguin Ireland, 25 St Stephen's Green, Dublin 2, Ireland (a division of Penguin Books Ltd)
Penguin Group (Australia), 707 Collins Street, Melbourne, Victoria 3008, Australia
(a division of Pearson Australia Group Pty Ltd)
Penguin Books India Pvt Ltd, 11 Community Centre, Panchsheel Park, New Delhi—110 017, India
Penguin Group (NZ), 67 Apollo Drive, Rosedale, Auckland 0632, New Zealand
(a division of Pearson New Zealand Ltd)
Penguin Books (South Africa), Rosebank Office Park, 181 Jan Smuts Avenue, Parktown North 2193, South Africa
Penguin China, B7 Jiaming Center, 27 East Third Ring Road North, Chaoyang District, Beijing 100020, China

Penguin Books Ltd, Registered Offices: 80 Strand, London WC2R 0RL, England

Original Title: Agatha Mistery: La perla del Bengala
Text by Sir Steve Stevenson
Original cover and illustrations by Stefano Turconi

English language edition copyright © 2013 Penguin Group (USA) Inc. Original edition published by Istituto
Geografico De Agostini S.p.A., Italy, 2010. © 2010 Atlantyca Dreamfarm s.r.l., Italy

International Rights © Atlantyca S.p.A. – via Leopardi 8, 20123 Milano, Italia –
foreignrights@atlantyca.it - www.atlantyca.com

Published in 2013 by Grosset & Dunlap, a division of Penguin Young Readers Group, 345 Hudson Street,
New York, New York 10014. GROSSET & DUNLAP is a trademark of Penguin Group (USA) Inc. Printed in the U.S.A

Library of Congress Cataloging-in-Publication Data is available.

10 9 8 7 6 5 4 3 2 1

ISBN 978-0-448-46219-6

PEARSON

ALWAYS LEARNING

Agatha

Girl of Mystery

The Pearl
of Bengal

by Sir Steve Stevenson
illustrated by Stefano Turconi

translated by Siobhan Kelly
adapted by Maya Gold

Grosset & Dunlap
An Imprint of Penguin Group (USA) Inc.

SECOND MISSION
Agents

Agatha
Twelve years old, an
aspiring mystery writer;
has a formidable memory

Dash
Agatha's cousin and student
at the private school Eye
International Detective Academy

Chandler
Butler and former boxer with impeccable British style

Watson
Obnoxious Siberian cat with the nose of a bloodhound

Uncle Rudyard
An adventurous wildlife photographer and animal wrangler

DESTINATION

India
New Delhi
The Bay of Bengal

OBJECTIVE

To find a priceless jewel, the legendary Pearl of Bengal, stolen from the temple of the goddess Kali in the Ganges River Delta.

The Investigation Begins . . .

*I*t was a Saturday afternoon in mid-October. Dashiell Mistery was elbowing his way through a sea of umbrellas that had popped up like mushrooms when a sudden downpour hit. Within minutes, all of London was drenched. The bustling city streets were as muddy and gray as a scene out of Dickens.

Fourteen years old and as thin as a rake, Dash was a typical teenage boy, except for his secret obsession. He was studying to be a detective, though he told everybody he met that he was pursuing an online degree in marketing.

Only a few family members knew the truth.

Among them was his extraordinary younger cousin, Agatha Mistery.

"Watch where you're going!" scolded a woman standing in front of a wig shop. In his rush, Dash had bumped into her, knocking her leather purse into a puddle. He scooped it up, shook it dry, and shoved it back into her hands.

"Here you go. Good as new!" he gasped, speeding away as she stood there sputtering. His best friends were waiting for him at the Hastings Street Bowling Alley, and if the church-tower clock he'd just passed was correct, he was already twenty minutes late.

As usual, Dash had taken his sweet time waking up. He'd slapped down his snooze-alarm several times, grabbed a slice of cold pizza while playing a rap mix he'd burned, and zoomed out of his penthouse apartment in Baker Palace without even checking the weather online.

Big mistake. Everybody in London knew

the city had only two kinds of weather: sun at intervals and rain at intervals.

The storm had caught Dash off guard. At first, he'd stood under an awning, hoping it was just a cloudburst. But the rain didn't let up—in fact, the longer he waited, the worse it got. He couldn't afford to lose any more time. He started to run, stopping only when he got stuck at a crosswalk. Now he was soaked from head to toe.

At Richmond Avenue, three blocks away, he hit another red light.

Panting and shivering, Dash huddled against a wrought-iron fence. What if his friends had given up on him and started their weekly challenge match? But they wouldn't do that without calling him first, would they?

A terrible thought slammed into his head. "Oh no!" he groaned, digging frantically through his pockets. Except for a few stray coins, they were empty.

He fingered the case where he kept his most precious gadget.

It was light. Too light.

Holding his breath, he reached in. There was nothing inside.

"Where did I put it? Where?" he cried out in panic.

Eye International, the famous detective school he attended, had one very strict rule: Never go anywhere without the tools of the trade.

This didn't mean the traditional investigator's kit (e.g., magnifying glass, bugging devices, spy cameras, and walkie-talkies). All of these functions and more were performed by a patented high-tech device called the EyeNet. The worst thing a student could do was to lose it.

If he couldn't find his EyeNet, Dash was in a sea of trouble. He kept patting his clothes in the pouring rain, waving his arms like an octopus. Meanwhile, the light had turned green, and a

new wave of bobbing umbrellas came at him.

Frozen in place, Dash pressed his palm on his forehead and tried to mentally reconstruct the events of the night before. He'd gone to Marshall's apartment, played video games for a couple hours, and gotten back home around midnight. Half asleep, he'd kicked back on the couch to watch some shows he'd recorded. This morning he'd woken up fully dressed, with the TV still on. Had he put his

EyeNet into its charger right next to the couch, like he did every night? He didn't remember doing it. Which could only mean . . .

"Marshall!" he shouted so loudly that passersby eyed him cautiously from underneath their umbrellas. "I left it at his apartment!"

Dash charged across Richmond Avenue without realizing the light had turned red. Horns honked and brakes squealed as taxicabs swerved

to avoid a collision. A policeman blew on his whistle, but Dash didn't bother to turn. Nothing mattered as much as getting his EyeNet back as soon as possible.

Five minutes later, he skidded into the Hastings Street Bowling Alley. Panting, he swiveled his head, looking for Marshall. Every lane was in use, and the sounds of heavy balls striking pins echoed through the cavernous room.

Dash vaulted over the seats where his friends were sitting without even saying hello. He leaped into the lane, grabbing Marshall's shoulder just as he let go of the ball. It swung wide and rolled into the gutter.

A big zero flashed on the scoreboard.

"Dash!" shouted Marshall. "That was a strike waiting to happen. You totally killed it!"

"Have you seen my . . . um . . . err . . . cell phone?"

"You left it at my place!"

"Thank God," the young detective said with a gulp. "Can I get it right now?"

"Look at you, Dash! You are beyond disgusting!" sniffed Alison, tossing her curls. She was wearing a bright pink designer sweater.

Marshall and the others snickered.

Dash was sure he did look disgusting. He could feel wet hair glued to his cheeks, his clothes dripped like a broken faucet, and he'd left muddy footprints streaked over the polished wood floor.

"Calm down, I brought it," said Marshall, rummaging through his backpack. "That thing is huge. Must be way overdue for an upgrade."

Dash grabbed it, heaving a sigh of relief. "Thanks, but no way I'd replace it! My dad gave me this phone, and it means a lot to me." He closed his fist over the EyeNet, trying to hide its array of buttons and flashing lights. Tapping a bowling ball, he added casually, "How about I

dry off by beating you all without mercy?"

"In your dreams," snorted Marshall.

Dash grinned. As he made his way toward the shoe rental counter, he quickly punched in his secret access code. The EyeNet had been in standby mode since late last night, and there might be urgent messages.

A high-pitched ring shattered the air. Just he suspected, the Eye International symbol was flashing insistently. There were eleven missed messages, all from his school!

Dash skimmed down to read the last message, and a desperate cry escaped his lips.

"*Kolkata?* In India? Oh God, what a mess! I need Agatha!"

His friends watched as he shot back out like a rocket. "What a weirdo!" sniffed Alison, but the others just shook their heads and went back to their game. They were used to the unpredictable ways of the Mistery family.

An Unexpected Reunion

The Mistery Estate was an ancient, lavender-roofed mansion on the edge of a park on the outskirts of London. Its high ceilings creaked with heavy oak beams. Whenever it rained, the grand old house seemed even gloomier. Windowpanes rattled inside their dark frames, and the wind seemed to haunt the large rooms, echoing down the long halls like the whispers of restless ghosts.

Luckily its residents were not easily frightened. For twelve-year-old Agatha Mistery, bright-eyed and petite, the sounds created a moody and magical atmosphere.

At that moment, Agatha lay on her canopy bed, listening to raindrops patter against her bedroom window, as though knocking to come in. After a few moments, she reached for her notebook and pen. "It's a perfect day for writing," she murmured to Watson, her white Siberian cat. "But let's have some inspiration first. What do you say to a spy movie?"

The cat let out a satisfied meow as Agatha scratched his favorite spot under the chin. Then he followed her down the back stairs to the screening room. While most home theaters boasted state-of-the-art sound systems and flat-screen TVs, the Misteries had a thing for outdated technologies. Agatha's parents, Rebecca and Arthur Conan Mistery, never took jets if there was a biplane or zeppelin handy.

Chandler, the Mistery Estate's jack-of-all-trades butler, was already fitting a take-up reel into the vintage projector, as if he'd read Agatha's mind.

Chandler was a former heavyweight boxer, with a square jaw and shoulders as broad as a redwood tree. As usual, he wore an immaculate dinner jacket, with his hair slicked back. "Which film have you chosen, Miss Agatha?" he asked politely as she entered.

She paused for a second. "I should brush up on Cold War spies for my new story, but I can't decide," she said, idly stroking the tip of her small upturned nose.

This simple gesture always helped her to focus her thoughts.

"What are you thinking, Miss?"

She searched for an answer. "There's also the indie film Mom and Dad sent me from San Francisco," she said. "It would be rude not to watch it before they get home."

Chandler cleared his throat. "They've taken a steamer to India, Miss Agatha," he replied. "They'll be there for at least a week."

"The international conference on renewable energy, right?"

The butler nodded, adjusting the projector's lens. "You'll have plenty of time to watch it before they return, Miss."

Agatha wasn't convinced. She turned toward Watson, who was nosing around through a dust-covered carton. "What are you up to, kitty?" she asked.

The cat jumped out of the carton and set his paw on a single film canister under the table—another gift from Mom and Dad. It had never been opened.

Chandler and Agatha exchanged a stunned glance.

"Apparently Watson has a thing for Alfred Hitchcock," she observed with a laugh.

She opened the canister and handed the butler a copy of Hitchcock's classic thriller *Rear Window*. "Decision made!"

"As you wish, Miss Agatha."

While Chandler patiently threaded the reel, Agatha pulled the dark velvet curtains closed, taking a seat in her favorite armchair. She wasn't one of those people who lounged on the couch munching popcorn, like some of her friends—or her cousin. She liked to take notes in the notebook that she always carried, jotting down quick descriptions of characters, furniture, costumes, and any other detail that caught her imagination.

Like every member of the Mistery family, Agatha had her eye on an eccentric career.

She wanted to be a writer.

More specifically, a mystery writer. The best in the world.

To that end, she spent her days reading novels, poring over old encyclopedias, flipping through magazines and newspapers, watching movies and documentaries, always on the lookout for interesting ideas for stories.

As soon as the room went dark and the opening credits started to roll, Agatha felt a shiver of excitement. She knew director Alfred Hitchcock was a master of suspense, and the opening shots of a city courtyard on a hot summer day made her wonder what terrible thing was about to take place there. A man in pajamas sat next to a window, his camera abandoned next to a stack of *Life* magazines. "A photographer," she murmured. "And his leg's in a cast, so . . ."

She felt a wet touch on her shoulder.

Who could it be?

She turned quickly.

"D-Dash?" she stammered.

"That's my name!"

"What are you doing here, cousin?"

"It's a disaster," he said, squirming to pat himself dry with a tissue. "Can you spare a couple of minutes?"

"Of course."

From the tone of his voice, she could already tell that a couple of minutes would not be enough.

Dash plunked down beside her. "My school's given me a new mission," he rattled. "I have to solve a really crazy case!" He broke off, leaping back out of his seat. "What in the world!?" he shouted. "What *is* that?!"

A dark shadow loomed over the screen. It was some sort of horrible monster with giant hooked claws.

"Are you jumpy or what, Dash?" laughed Agatha. "Look closer. It's just Watson's shadow. He stepped in front of the projector!"

"Oh—oh, are you sure? That cat's trying to kill me! I could have died of fright!"

There was a lot of bad blood between Dash and Watson.

Agatha stood up, waving her arms to get Chandler's attention. He snapped on the lights and turned off the projector.

"Sorry, Agatha." Dash stared guiltily at the blank screen. "I didn't mean to interrupt your screening . . ."

"Tell me everything."

The young detective started to pace back and forth as he filled her in. He couldn't be sure that his phone wasn't tapped—his professors were experts at spyware—so he'd come in person to the Mistery Estate. He didn't want anybody at Eye International to know how much Agatha helped him with solving the cases he was assigned.

"Got it," said Agatha. "Where are we being sent this time?"

"It's a village in Sundarbans National Park, near Kolkata."

"You're kidding me." Agatha flinched. "My parents are in India, too. That's too close for comfort!"

"Excuse my correction, Miss Agatha," Chandler interjected. No one ever noticed his

light, discreet steps. "Mr. and Mrs. Mistery are in the capital city, New Delhi, in western India," he explained. "Kolkata is in the east, hundreds of miles away."

"Yes, of course, Chandler," Agatha said, nodding. "But we may have to fly through New Delhi. What will we do if we run into them?"

Just as Dash hid his cousin's help from his professors, Agatha had never told her parents that she accompanied Dash on his missions around the world.

"Let's plan a surprise for them," suggested Dash.

Agatha pursed her lips, doubtful. "What sort of surprise?"

"Simple. Once we've solved the case, we'll go visit them in New Delhi. I bet they'll jump for joy to see us! What do you think?"

Chandler gave a small nod of agreement.

"I have to admit, that's not a bad thought,"

said Agatha, twisting a lock of her short, blond hair. "All right, let's do it!"

She sent the butler to pack while she and Dash went to her room to download mission data.

They clicked on the main file, and a familiar face with a mustache and bowler hat filled the screen.

It was Agent UM60, professor of Investigation Techniques.

Dash's cheeks flushed instantly.

"I'll be brief, Agent DM14," the professor

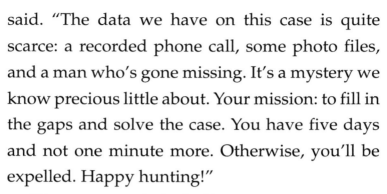

said. "The data we have on this case is quite scarce: a recorded phone call, some photo files, and a man who's gone missing. It's a mystery we know precious little about. Your mission: to fill in the gaps and solve the case. You have five days and not one minute more. Otherwise, you'll be expelled. Happy hunting!"

The message clicked off.

"Interesting," said Agatha.

"You mean *terrifying*," said Dash, who looked very pale.

The girl clicked open the file containing the recorded phone call. The audio signal was very bad, and they had to replay it several times to understand some parts.

"Someone's inside the house . . . KSSSHH KSSSHH . . . They've picked the lock, I hear feet on the stairs . . . KSSSHH KSSSHH . . . They're coming toward my door, I know what they're after—the pearl! The pearl! KSSSHH KSSSHH . . . If anything happens

to me, tell my dear friend . . . KSSSHH KSSSHH . . . Deshpande! . . . BEEP-BEEP-BEEP-BEEP . . .

Agatha's eyes glowed with excitement. "First off, we need to discover whose voice that is. Then we can start reconstructing exactly what happened. You agree, Dash?"

White-faced, Dash rubbed his temples as if he'd just gotten the world's biggest headache.

Off to Kolkata

*T*he only nonstop to Kolkata was a red-eye from Heathrow at 10:00 p.m. The Mistery cousins were glad to have plenty of prep time.

They split up the tasks. Chandler booked their flights and took care of all the travel details, Dash pored over the files his school had attached, and Agatha went to the Mistery Estate's huge library to investigate India.

"If memory serves," she told Dash, "one of our relatives wrote an article about Bengal tigers for *National Geographic*."

"Did you pull that out of one of your famous memory drawers?" Dash smirked. He was always

cracking jokes about Agatha's amazing memory. He paused for a moment, then stuttered, "Wait! What? Did you just say . . . *tigers?!*"

"I did," she said calmly. "The Sundarbans region has the largest population of man-eaters in the whole world!"

Dash shook his head and turned back to his file. "As if that obnoxious cat weren't bad enough, now we're dealing with man-eating tigers!" he groaned.

Like her parents, Agatha preferred old-fashioned technologies. While Dash surfed the net with his EyeNet, she rolled a ladder around the high shelves of the oak-paneled library, pulling down a dozen leather-bound volumes on the history and religions of India. Even at first glance, it looked like a very complicated subject.

Next, she searched for the issue of *National Geographic* with the photo spread on Bengal tigers. "I was right!" she told Dash. "His name

is Rudyard Mistery! He's a nature photographer, and a very brave one, from the looks of these close-ups."

"Oh great," said her cousin. He didn't sound happy.

Agatha studied a shot of a snarling male tiger's face. "Looks like he used an extreme telephoto lens, like the one in *Rear Window*."

She and Dash went to look at the Mistery family tree, a gigantic world map marked with residences, occupations, and family relationships of every known member of the Mistery clan. "Here he is, *Uncle Rudyard*," she exclaimed. "Oh, and what good luck—he lives in Kolkata!"

She picked up the phone and dialed his number. "I hope he's working in his darkroom. It's a four-and-a-half-hour time difference," she noted. "I hope he can give us a hand!"

From the other end of the line, a hearty voice

boomed, "Mistery Photo, hello there. Who's calling from London?" It was Uncle Rudyard.

The conversation went for a good half an hour. By the time Rudyard finally hung up, Agatha's ears were smoking. "That uncle of ours can talk a blue streak," she told Dash, slightly breathless. "But he's already gotten 'an old chum' to set up a visitors' permit for Sundarbans National Park. And he has a peculiar request."

"Of course he does, he's a Mistery! What is it this time?"

"He asked if any of us can fly a plane."

Just then, Chandler entered the room with his usual discretion. "If I can be of service, Miss Agatha, many years ago I took flying lessons."

"Excellent, Chandler," she replied. "Add your aviation equipment to our luggage."

The butler didn't bat an eye. "As you wish, Miss," he said. "Dinner is served."

They went to the ancestral dining room and

sat at a long Louis XIV table, set with the Mistery family's best china. Chandler had even set out the silver cutlery and linen napkins with the family monogram.

He served the cousins a perfectly cooked sole meunière, which they wolfed down in no time. Dash took seconds of everything, and thirds of the roasted potatoes.

"What did you learn from the files, Dash?" asked Agatha, digging a spoon into her chocolate mousse.

"There was a theft," mumbled Dash with his mouth full.

"The pearl in the phone message?"

Dash nodded. "Not just any pearl. The world-famous Pearl of Bengal."

Agatha touched the tip of her nose. "Hmm, I read something about that . . . A Hindu temple half buried in the jungle, with an ancient statue of the goddess Kali . . ." She paused for a moment.

"Kali was holding the pearl in the palm of her hand, am I right?"

Dash was no longer astonished by Agatha's amazing mnemonic talents. "You opened the right drawer, cousin. The village is called Chotoka. It's on the delta of the Ganges River. Very remote," he added. "The website called it 'inaccessible.'"

"Anything else?" she pressed.

"On the night of the theft, the old custodian, Amitav Chandra, disappeared. He was the only one who knew which ten of a hundred keys opened the doors to the sanctuary of the goddess Kali. It was his voice we heard on the recording."

"Abduction or murder?"

"Nobody knows yet," Dash replied, sounding uncertain. "There are no police in Sundarbans National Park, only the forest guard, led by Captain Deshpande."

"The 'dear friend' in the message?"

"Exactly." Dash nodded as he laid out photographs he had downloaded.

Agatha and Chandler stared in silence at the wild mangrove jungle surrounding the temple. Chotoka village seemed to be swallowed by bright green foliage. There were no roads around it, only some winding dirt paths and wide waterways navigated by fishermen in small wooden boats. Fortunately among the thatched huts was a large bungalow with a hand-painted sign reading TIGER HOTEL.

"Uncle Rudyard suggested we stay there," Agatha murmured to her cousin. "Back to our case. Who are the suspects?" she asked.

"I don't know," spluttered Dash, holding a grape halfway to his mouth. "That's all there was in the file. We've got nothing to go on!"

Agatha glanced at the clock and took the situation in hand. "To recap, twenty-four hours ago, a rare pearl of incalculable value was

stolen from a Hindu temple."

She picked up a photo of the precious pearl. It was a perfect sphere, nearly black, with silvery highlights.

"Just before the theft occurred, the custodian, Amitav Chandra, called Eye International from his home," she said, closing her eyelids. "Someone broke into his home, forced open the door of the temple, stole the Bengal Pearl, and then . . ."

". . . killed Mr. Chandra?" Dash guessed, sounding worried.

"We don't know that," said Agatha, laying her hands on the table. "We only know that he's disappeared into thin air. But in his phone call, Chandra said to contact Deshpande, the captain of the forest guard. This Captain Deshpande should be able to give us more information about suspects once we arrive in the village," she concluded.

At that moment, Chandler started clearing dessert.

Agatha stopped him. "Leave that, Chandler," she told him. "Dash will finish it. Go pack some sunscreen and mosquito repellent. We're going to need it!"

"Of course, Miss Agatha." The butler nodded.

Minutes later, they were in a limousine speeding to Heathrow Airport.

Dash had told his parents that he'd be staying at Agatha's for a few days to prepare for an important and difficult exam, which was almost the truth. To save time, he had not gone back to his penthouse. He'd stick with the clothes he was wearing. In place of the hair gel he usually used on his floppy dark hair, he'd tried olive oil.

"Oh, the mosquitoes are going to love you," laughed Agatha as they boarded the Air India jet. As always, she had Watson's traveling case in one hand.

"Don't mock my style," said Dash, taking a seat by the window and burrowing under a blanket. Before they even took off, he was out like a light.

For the first hour, Agatha read guidebooks about Kolkata and Sundarbans National Park. Then she, too, fell into a deep sleep, with Watson curled up in her lap.

Chandler didn't even close his eyes. The seats were too narrow for him to make himself comfortable, so he passed his time poring over a dog-eared flight instruction manual, making notes with a highlighter pen.

They landed in Kolkata the following morning. Agatha was as fresh as a daisy, while Dash had dark circles under his eyes. He couldn't stop yawning.

"One of these days you'll make it into the *Guinness Book of World Records*," Agatha teased him cheerfully as they rode the escalator to the

baggage claim. "World champion sleeper!"

Dash gave his millionth yawn in reply. "It's changing time zones that destroys me," he moaned.

"Right." Agatha smirked. "Four and a half hours' difference isn't that much."

"It's the extra half hour!"

They picked up their luggage in no time. Chandler showed their passports to the customs officials, and they emerged into the airport's central atrium.

It was like a miniature city, crowded and bustling with color. Glittering displays of designer cosmetics sat next to narrow stands selling orange and pink silks, silver bracelets, and beaded necklaces. Women of all shapes and sizes walked past, wrapped in brightly patterned saris. Some of the men wore traditional white or brown clothing and turbans, while others wore business suits.

In the midst of the crowded bazaar, they spotted a young Indian with bulging calf muscles waving a sign that said RASHID'S RICKSHAW— FASTEST IN KOLKATA!

"The only thing missing is a snake charmer," joked Dash.

"See, that's where you're wrong," a cheerful voice boomed behind him. "I can charm anything, even a cobra."

They turned to see a broad-shouldered man with unruly blond hair, a ruddy tan, and a welcoming grin. He looked about thirty years old, and in

spite of a little potbelly, he looked very fit. In his beige shorts, tan shirt, and hiking boots, he was the very image of an adventurer.

"Welcome to India, the most exciting place on the planet!" exclaimed Rudyard Mistery.

Uncle Rudyard's Folly

After vigorously shaking Chandler's hand, hugging his niece and nephew, and cracking a few jokes about Dash's olive-oiled hair, Uncle Rudyard reached into his camera bag for an aviator cap and goggles. "Okay, which one of you knows how to pilot a plane?" he asked without preamble. Apparently he couldn't wait to get back to the wilds of Bengal.

"I, er, failed my pilot's license three times," Chandler began, rubbing his jaw. "But I know how to steer with a joystick and check the altimeter . . ."

"Excellent! Good man!" Uncle Rudyard said,

thumping his shoulder. "They won't let us take off without a backup pilot!"

The butler solemnly put on the aviator cap, tinted goggles, and an oversize brown leather jacket he'd brought with him from London.

"You're a vision, big man!" Rudyard Mistery grinned. "Who's going to argue with *that?*"

Agatha laughed heartily, but Dash looked uncertain.

"Don't you think this uncle of ours is being a bit optimistic?" he whispered in his cousin's ear as they walked to the hangar where their private plane was waiting. "Chandler did say he failed three times."

"Uncle Rudyard's terrific! A real force of nature," Agatha said, glowing.

Dash rolled his eyes. Apparently Rudyard could charm cousins as well as snakes.

Suitcases in hand, they went out through a side door and walked across the hot tarmac, passing a small fleet of maintenance vehicles unloading luggage from planes. Uncle Rudyard stopped next to a hangar to greet a few grease-stained mechanics in Hindi and English. Then he pointed to the flight inspector's office.

"Come on, big man!" he invited Chandler. "Let's go convince them you're an RAF ace!"

A few minutes passed. Agatha reached down to stroke Watson's paw, which the cat had stuck out through the mesh of his carrier.

"Don't worry, I'll let you out soon!" she consoled him.

"Fine with me if you don't," grumbled Dash. "I'd almost forgotten that lousy beast!"

As Agatha glared, the others emerged from the office, flashing thumbs-ups.

As soon as Uncle Rudyard gestured proudly toward his plane, the children understood why he needed a backup pilot.

It was a gigantic yellow Canadair with bright red stripes, almost entirely covered in stickers. It was sixty feet long with a ninety-foot wingspan, an amphibious beast capable of landing on a jungle runway or body of water with equal ease.

"That's my honey. She used to be a water bomber for fighting wildfires, but I had her refitted for photo expeditions," explained

Rudyard Mistery proudly. "Isn't she beautiful?"

"What a spectacular plane!" Agatha cried. "Mom and Dad would adore it. They're nuts about vintage aircraft!"

Chandler just stared at the plane, sweating profusely in his leather jacket.

They climbed into the Canadair's roomy cabin and immediately noted that it was furnished like a hiker's cabin. There was a hammock, a gas stove, food supplies (mostly rice and canned

tuna), bottled water, fishing rods, tripods, and waterproof camera equipment.

"I don't just shoot tigers, you know," their uncle explained, showing them his scuba gear. "The Irrawaddy dolphins migrate back to the Ganges from the Bay of Bengal at this time of year. I want to get some underwater shots."

"What's in those colored vials?" asked Dash.

"Snake serum."

"You mean, to treat snakebites?"

Rudyard shook his head. "To attract snakes so I can shoot close-ups."

Dash's eyes got big. "P-p-poisonous snakes?"

"Deadly." Rudyard grinned.

Dash's knees started to shake. They shook even more when Uncle Rudyard and Chandler strapped themselves into the copilot seats, and the seaplane's propellers began to spin.

It was the worst takeoff the boy could remember.

The Canadair swung back and forth, lurching wildly from left to right, thumping and creaking. Dash grabbed hold of a large metal handle, while Agatha calmly gazed out the window.

When they finally reached cruising altitude in the clear skies above Kolkata, Uncle Rudyard entrusted the stick to the butler. "Put her on a bearing of one twenty south," he shouted in incomprehensible pilot jargon. "I'm going to go chat with the youngsters."

Nervous as he was, Chandler kept his eye on the control panel, obeying him to the letter.

"Now, Agatha. What can you tell me about your investigation?" asked Uncle Rudyard as he relaxed in his hammock. Watson jumped onto his belly, where he was welcomed with plenty of cuddles.

"It's a tough one," replied the girl, tugging on her cousin's sleeve. "Dash can fill you in." She tugged harder. "Right, Agent DM14?"

"Uh, me?"

"You're the detective!" Agatha grinned. "Go on, lazy, tell him!"

She knew there was only one way to calm down her cousin. In fact, as he recapped the details of their mission, he started to loosen up, bit by bit. At one point, he pulled out his EyeNet to show Rudyard the pictures of Chotoka, the Temple of Kali, and the magnificent missing black pearl.

"What an amazing doohickey!" Rudyard Mistery enthused. "Go back a few frames. Can you zoom in?"

Dash zoomed in on the image of Deshpande, captain of the forest guard.

Rudyard nodded. "I know him. He was mauled by a tiger last year. He was an expert at tracking down poachers, but he hasn't been the same since that bite on the leg."

"Mr. Chandra told us to contact him," Agatha said. "Uncle, what can you tell us about the villagers of Chotoka?"

Rudyard Mistery shrugged. "They're mostly fishermen and rice farmers, except for the priests in the Temple of Kali, the pilgrims who worship there, and a few ecotourists who come for the wildlife," he replied. "The villagers live simple lives, but they're crazy about movies, cell phones, and the Internet! Don't you find that an odd contradiction?"

The children nodded. Uncle Rudyard had a way of putting everyone at ease. Suddenly he jumped up from the hammock and shouted, "Doing all right there, big man? You can begin the descent. We're almost there!"

Dash and Agatha grinned.

"Look out the window," said Rudyard, pointing to the enormous green delta of the Ganges River. "They call the Sundarbans 'land of tides,' where land and water mingle together in little islands that are continually being born and disappearing."

The scenery was breathtakingly beautiful. Even Dash gazed down at it, speechless.

"Fortunately, the monsoon season's over. We wouldn't have been able to land my plane in those storms," said their uncle. "And the village streets would be soaked."

Leaving both cousins to stare at the view, he rejoined Chandler in the cockpit. "Hand her over

to me," he announced happily. "Prepare for a landing!"

As Chandler got up to sit in the passenger seat, he felt something rubbery, like a bicycle tire. Then it moved. Whipping off his goggles, he stared at the control panel as a large, coppery snake slithered underneath it.

Chandler jumped up so fast he hit his head on the ceiling. "I fear we have a big problem!" he shouted, maintaining his sense of formality. "There's a snake on the plane!"

As Rudyard angled in for a landing, pandemonium broke out on the Canadair. A terrified Dash dived headfirst into the hammock, while Agatha tried to grab Watson, whose bristling tail made it clear he did not like big snakes.

The Canadair lurched and rocked, slamming onto the surface of the Ganges with a great spray of wake. It bobbed up and down like an oversize

tub toy, finally stopping in front of the rickety dock at Chotoka. Villagers clustered around to see what was happening and stare at the strangers who'd made such a clamorous entrance.

Without even cutting the engines, Rudyard Mistery shot out of his seat like a lightning bolt. He spotted the snake coiled under an oxygen tank and started moving his fingers like a magician. Then he made a sudden swift lunge, grabbing the snake right behind its big head.

"Well, hello there, big guy!" he said, gently stroking it between the eyes. The snake, more than a yard long, writhed in his arms. "What made you stow away on my plane, little python? If you wanted to take a vacation, you just had to ask!"

Terrified, Dash clung to Chandler. At the same moment, they asked, "Is it poisonous?"

"Not in the least!" Rudyard said with a smile. "He'll just crush you to death."

Dash brandished a barbecue fork. "It's us or him!" he cried.

"Calm down, calm down. He's just a young fellow. They can get to be twenty feet long." Uncle Rudyard opened the plane's rear door and carefully placed the squirming reptile into the water. "There you go. Swim home to Mama."

Chuckling, he looked at his passengers. "The situation is under control."

Dash put down the fork, and Chandler

exhaled with relief. Agatha looked out the open door, realizing the muddy bank was a good thirty yards away.

"Ready for a nice swim?" she squeaked.

"Not with that snake and his twenty-foot mama!" Dash shuddered.

"No worries!" said Rudyard. "We'll use my inflatable raft."

Agatha smiled. Uncle Rudyard might be a little bit crazy, but he had an answer for everything!

Deshpande's List

*T*he villagers craned their necks to watch as Rudyard helped the two kids clamber onto the inflatable raft. Chandler's bulk nearly sank it. By the time he'd rowed the small group to the muddy bank, the villagers had begun to disperse, their faces disappointed. Soon the bend in the river was empty, the humid silence broken only by the chirping of waterbirds.

"Uncle, what were those people muttering about?" asked Dash, who could not speak a word of Bengali.

"When they saw us arrive in the plane, they thought we had found the missing man."

"You mean Amitav Chandra, the temple's custodian?" Agatha clarified.

Rudyard nodded. "Sounds like they're still holding out hope of finding him." He shook his head, tying the raft to the dock. "Between you and me, I think it'll be like finding a needle in a haystack." He sighed. "Sundarbans National Park is vast. Plenty of places to hide a body. And plenty of pythons and crocodiles to finish the job if he isn't already dead."

"Why don't you do an aerial search in your seaplane?" suggested Agatha. "Something tells me he's safe and sound somewhere!"

Dash frowned, suspicious. "But what if he's guilty? What if Chandra stole the Pearl of Bengal himself and faked everything so he could run off with it?"

Agatha picked up Watson, who was watching a shorebird with interest. "Dash, your hypothesis doesn't hold up," she said firmly. "If Mr. Chandra

wanted to disappear with the loot, why would he notify Eye International?"

The conversation was cut short by Chandler, who pointed toward the embankment. "We've got company, Miss Agatha."

They turned to see a burly man with a large mustache waiting for them on the steps to the village gate. He was wearing a camouflage

uniform and cap, and leaned on a bamboo cane that looked too thin to support him.

"Good afternoon, Captain Deshpande!" Uncle Rudyard waved across the distance.

"Professor Mistery, what brings you back to Chotoka? I thought you were offshore taking pictures of dolphins!"

Agatha noted a curious tone in the captain's voice, as if he was displeased to have visitors.

A split second later, he added, "Come to my office and show me your permits. I don't want anyone wasting my time." He turned and limped away.

Rudyard reached into his camera bag, handing authorized permits to Dash and Agatha. "Deshpande is a sharp, stubborn man," he said grimly. "He'll subject you to an interrogation to find out exactly why you're here."

Agatha stroked her nose, grinning. "Well, then, we'll tell him the truth!"

"Wh-what?" stammered Dash.

"Does that bother you, cousin?"

"But—but . . . you want to share everything Eye International gave us?"

"Of course, the whole truth." The girl's eyes shone with cleverness. "Minus one particular detail," she added.

"What?" the young detective asked her, excited. "Which detail?"

Even Chandler raised an eyebrow.

Agatha dropped her voice. "We can't mention Mr. Chandra's phone call," she explained. "It's the one thing nobody in the village knows about, not even the thief. It will be the ace up our sleeve!"

And so it was.

They told Captain Deshpande that they were investigating on orders from a reputable international agency and would like his full cooperation. They wanted to know all the details from the current investigation: suspects,

evidence, and whatever clues the forest guard had obtained.

The captain filed their permits in the cabinet behind his desk, gazing at them with a smirk. "So you're my reinforcements?" he asked Agatha and Dash. "Aren't you two a bit young to be detectives?"

"They're extremely bright kids, Captain," Uncle Rudyard interjected. Until then, he had remained silent with his fingers linked behind his head.

"They're your niece and nephew, so of course you'd speak well of them, Professor Mistery," he replied curtly. "But I'm not convinced. I want to see their credentials."

Dash was ready for this. Punching a secret code into his EyeNet, he handed the device to the captain.

"Use the cursor to scroll down the screen. You'll find all the credentials you need regarding

me and the agency I represent," he said firmly.

The onscreen résumé was a detailed list of Dash's solved cases, designed to impress anyone at first glance.

Too bad it was a fake!

Quite a brilliant one . . . but would it bear up under the scrutiny of the captain Uncle Rudyard had called "stubborn" and "sharp"?

The anxious silence in the small office was disturbed only by the whir of a creaky, slow fan and the buzzing of gnats. As Deshpande read, a single drop of sweat formed on his forehead and slowly made its way down his cheek, coming to rest in his mustache.

"Very hot today, isn't it?" he said, unbuttoning his collar. He pushed the EyeNet back to Dash and leaned forward. "Right, then, you have my permission to investigate," he said. "What do my young colleagues wish to know?"

The hoax had worked to perfection!

While her cousin shoved the EyeNet back into its case with a private sigh of relief, Agatha started to hammer Deshpande with questions. "Let's start with your suspects. Who are they?"

"I've lived in this village for over thirty years and know all of the villagers well," the captain replied. "Therefore I have excluded everyone who was friendly with old Mr. Chandra, including myself."

"Who's left, then?" Agatha pressed him, opening her notebook to a blank page.

Deshpande paused. Starting with the thumb on his right hand, he started to count them off. "Brahman Sangali, who never agreed with Chandra about how the temple should be run." He raised his index finger. "The pair of Spanish tourists staying at the Tiger Hotel. They have a record of thefts in other parts of the world."

When he came to his third finger, he stopped.

"Well?" Dash blurted. "Who else?"

"You promised full cooperation, Captain," Agatha reminded him.

Deshpande sighed deeply. "You must understand, this isn't easy for me . . . Do you know Naveen Chandra, the famous Bollywood actor?"

"Don't you mean Hollywood, sir?" Dash corrected him.

Agatha cleared her throat. "Dash, my dear, Bollywood is the biggest movie industry in the world. It's the Indian equivalent of Hollywood," she explained.

"Oh, sorry. I didn't realize . . ." Dash blushed.

"The answer is no," Agatha interrupted. "We haven't heard of Naveen Chandra. Who is he, Captain?"

"Our prime suspect in the theft of the pearl," the official said with a heavy sigh. "Naveen Chandra is Amitav Chandra's son!"

Everyone was astonished. For the first time,

Agatha pulled her pen from the page.

Rudyard was the first to respond. "We understand your pain, as a friend of the family," he tried to reassure Captain Deshpande, "but tell me, these suspects, are they in jail? Have you put them behind bars for interrogation?"

"The law doesn't allow me to take them into custody, Professor Mistery," the captain replied, sounding miserable. "I've taken their statements and ordered them not to leave the village, at least until we find my dear friend Amitav, who I pray is still alive."

"Very wise," said Agatha. "But what makes Naveen Chandra the prime suspect?"

"He returned to Chotoka ten days ago, insisting he had to make peace with his father, who's never forgiven him for pursuing an acting career," explained the captain. "On the afternoon before Amitav disappeared, they had a huge fight. That night, several people claimed they

saw Naveen prowling around his father's house. None of the witnesses could be sure it was him, because it was pitch-black."

"So you don't have a reliable witness and can't incriminate him," Dash deduced. He had hoped they'd arrived on the brink of solving the case.

"Thank you for your assistance, Captain Deshpande." Agatha rose from her chair. "To help you pursue this matter, we have three simple requests."

"Of course, Miss."

"First, we need all the suspects' sworn statements."

"I'll make you a copy, he said, calling an officer into his office and handing him the papers What else?"

"We'd like your permission to question them further."

"Agreed. And the last thing?"

"To conduct a thorough investigation, we need to examine Amitav Chandra's home, and the Temple of Kali."

Captain Deshpande shook his head. "Unfortunately I cannot allow that," he said stiffly. "Both locations are under lockdown by the forest guard until further notice."

"But—" Dash started.

Agatha held up her hand. Instead of arguing, she grabbed the copies from the returning officer and shook the captain's hand firmly. He rose to his feet with the aid of his bamboo cane.

"That's all for now, Captain Deshpande," she said with a disarming smile. "If you need to reach us, we'll be at the Tiger Hotel."

High Tea at the Tiger Hotel

*C*hotoka's main street—really more of a wide, muddy path—cut the village in half. At the far end loomed the Temple of Kali, nestled into a distant green hillside. On both sides perched a jumble of houses and open-air shops, where women and children in brightly colored clothes worked in silence—except for the loud chatter of monkeys and tropical birdcalls. Most of the buildings were wood and bamboo with thatched roofs.

"They build them on stilts because of the danger of flooding, right, Uncle?" Dash asked as they walked down the street, dodging puddles.

"Not just that, Dash. It's also to discourage visits from dangerous animals."

"Like . . . ?"

"Oh, scorpions, snakes, crocodiles, leopards, tigers!" Rudyard replied cheerfully. Then he closed his eyes and breathed deeply, inhaling the scents of the jungle. "This is a magical spot!" he exclaimed. "Can't you just smell the adventure around us?"

The others just stared at him. His enthusiasm seemed out of place after their tense conversation with Captain Deshpande.

"What I'd love to smell is a nice cup of tea," said Agatha, checking her watch. It was a little past five in the evening—time for high tea in London.

They arrived at the cast-iron gate of the Tiger Hotel. The two-story bungalow formed an L shape around an orderly English garden. There was no need to ring the bell under the hotel sign,

because an Indian girl, a bit younger than Agatha, was already hanging over the gate waiting for them.

"Your luggage, if you please," she said politely in English. Taking the wheeled suitcase and bags from Chandler's huge hands, she loaded them onto her shoulders and headed toward the front desk.

"Wait! What's your name?" Agatha called after her, but she'd already vanished between garden hedges. Resigned, Agatha told the butler, "Please give that girl a big tip."

"As you wish, Miss Agatha."

They went through the gate and walked down a white gravel path. Tourists sat at tables around the garden, and Agatha's eagle eye took them in at a glance: an old gentleman in a linen suit reading the newspaper through pince-nez glasses, a dark-haired young couple conversing intently, and finally a handsome Indian man in

a blue satin tunic who sat with a cigar, watching the smoke rings he blew rise up into the air.

"Three out of these four we know," whispered Agatha, who had already glanced though the folder of witness statements and photos of suspects.

"The two Spaniards and Naveen Chandra," replied Dash, whispering into his cousin's ear. "But who's the dapper old gent with the *London Times*?"

The mysterious figure puzzled them both. Why had Captain Deshpande not mentioned this mustached man who looked so quintessentially British? Was he a local or just passing through as a tourist? He didn't look like someone who'd come here for wilderness treks.

"We'll find out soon enough," Agatha promised shrewdly as they stepped inside.

The reception area consisted of a simple counter with a half-filled guest register and

several posters of tigers on the wall. "I took that beauty's portrait last fall," Uncle Rudyard said proudly, pointing to an especially fierce-looking beast.

"Welcome to the Tiger Hotel, gentlemen, Miss," a cheerful Indian boy greeted them, bowing with his hands clasped in front of his chest. "How many rooms will you require?"

"Two double rooms, preferably with mosquito nets and a ceiling fan," replied Agatha as she bowed back in the same way.

Uncle Rudyard squirmed. "Not for me, niece," he said. "I won't need a hotel room. I always bunk right in my plane!"

"Awesome, Uncle!" Dash said with a grin. "Is there room for me, too?"

Agatha gave him a nudge in the ribs. "You need to stay here with me," she said. "You're on a case, remember? Besides, you don't want to be sharing his plane with a water snake." Dash became quiet.

She turned back to the receptionist. "Change of plans. Do you have any triples?"

"Upstairs?" asked Dash.

The boy passed Chandler the keys to Room 16 and collected their passports. "Take their bags, Parama!" he ordered the girl who'd met them at the gate. She stopped playing with Watson and took off up the stairs like a whirlwind.

"Perfect," said Agatha, satisfied. "Now we can go settle in and then . . . a nice cup of tea!"

"I have to unload a few things from the plane," said Uncle Rudyard. "I was wondering if Chandler could give me a hand with some of the heavy equipment."

"Of course," replied Agatha. "We'll see you at dinner!"

Rudyard took Chandler's stiff arm and pulled him outside, thumping him on the back. "Come on, big man! Time to unstiffen the old upper lip—you're in India now! We're going to have all

sorts of adventures!" they heard him say as the two walked away.

"What a funny pair!" Agatha giggled. "One never talks and one never shuts up!"

"They'd make a great comedy act," Dash agreed.

They went upstairs to their rooms to freshen up, giving little Parama a tip. She thanked them with a shy nod as Dash checked the corners for scorpions.

When they returned to the garden for tea, they noticed that the Spaniards and the distinguished gentleman had already left their tables.

Only Naveen Chandra remained.

While Dash scarfed down a plateful of cookies, Agatha opened the file and speed-read the famous Bollywood actor's statement. This was another of her incredible skills. She scanned all eight typed pages in less than a minute. As soon as she finished, she took a sip from a

steaming cup of Darjeeling tea and announced, "I'm ready!"

"Ready for what?" Dash stared at her, his mouth covered in chocolate.

"I want to question Naveen Chandra and verify his version of events." Agatha tapped her finger on Deshpande's file and then slid it inside her purse. "Are you coming, or would you prefer to make yourself sick by inhaling more of those cookies?" she asked with a smile.

"Um, sure, yes, I'm coming!" he answered, licking his lips.

Naveen Chandra had long, smooth black hair and luminous peacock-blue eyes. He was movie-star handsome but seemed ill at ease. He was still blowing puffs of cigar smoke and staring distractedly off into space.

He regarded the two cousins without interest. "Sorry, kids, I've run out of signed photos," he

said. "If you want an autograph, you'll have to bring me a paper and pen."

"That's all right, Mr. Chandra." Agatha sat down at the table. Still holding her cup of tea, she said quietly, "We were so sorry to hear about your situation. We know how much you love your father."

"Oh really?" he replied bitterly. "You're the only ones who think so!" Grinding out his cigar, he threw a quick glance at the kids. "Thanks to

Captain Deshpande, the whole village thinks I'm a thief and a murderer!"

"It's like being a prisoner, isn't it?" Agatha said, imagining herself in his shoes. "You can't leave the Tiger Hotel, you can't help with the search, you can't go back home. You're just stuck here, with nothing to do but worry!"

Struck by her compassion, the star began venting his feelings more freely. "I came back after all these years to bring my townspeople a bit of happiness," he said. "I wanted to start a school, build a new movie theater. The money that comes with success like mine can work miracles."

"But it can't buy your father's respect." Agatha nodded, sipping her tea.

Naveen Chandra looked at her. "That's the truth," he admitted. "I swear I've tried everything, but he's ashamed of me. He's a deeply religious man. He said that my *atman*, my inner spirit, was

corrupted by money and fame, and he wanted no part of it. He didn't recognize me as his son anymore."

"Did you argue a lot?" Dash asked, listening attentively. "I fight with my mom all the time. She says I'm a slacker and a hopeless waste of good groceries."

For the first time in days, Naveen Chandra laughed. "Three days ago, right before Daddyji disappeared, he shouted at me in the street! I haven't seen him since." His expression turned grim and he whispered, "I didn't steal the Pearl of Bengal. What use would I have for it? I'm already incredibly rich!"

"But several people saw you outside your father's house on the night of the theft," Agatha pressed. "What were you doing there?"

Naveen Chandra jumped to his feet. "That's a lie!" he roared. "I went to bed early that night. The boy at reception can tell you! He was at the

front desk when I went upstairs!"

"But you could have sneaked back out through the hotel window," Agatha pointed out. "It's just a short drop to the ground."

This infuriated him even more. "Are you joking?" he cried. "You think I'm guilty, too!"

He was about to storm away with both fists clenched when the Tiger Hotel gate creaked open. Two forest guards and a fisherman entered. Behind them stood Captain Deshpande.

Naveen Chandra stood in the middle of the garden, watching as they approached.

"Is this the man you saw?" Deshpande asked the fisherman.

The fisherman stared at the handsome Bollywood actor for a moment, then nodded vigorously. "Yes, I'm positive! I saw this man pick the lock on the custodian's house and sneak inside. Yes, yes, it was definitely him, Captain!"

Agatha and Dash watched as Naveen

Chandra was handcuffed. He didn't resist. The two guards escorted him into the street and toward the prison.

Captain Deshpande took a seat at the cousins' table, his expression serene. "Well, I won't need any reinforcements now, my friends," he said, stirring the gravel with his bamboo cane. "I finally found a reliable witness. That fisherman is Amitav Chandra's neighbor. He's just returned from a two-day trip up the river," he explained. "If only I had been able to question him earlier!"

With a small smile, Agatha opened her purse. "Do you want the witness statements back, Captain?"

He shrugged. "Keep them, Miss, keep them!" he said with a happy sigh, ambling slowly away. "This case is closed!"

Agatha wasn't so sure.

Something Doesn't Add Up

*T*hey dined that night on the Tiger Hotel's rooftop terrace, enjoying a spicy shrimp curry and charcoal-grilled naan bread. A fiery sunset lit up the sky, its colors reflected in the still waters of the Ganges. The night sounds of the forest made the scene even more exotic.

"But the case isn't closed at all," Agatha told Uncle Rudyard and Chandler. "The captain has put Naveen Chandra in jail, but his father's still missing and so is the pearl."

"You don't think he's guilty, Miss Agatha?" asked the butler, his broad shoulders aching from

carrying Rudyard's heavy scuba equipment.

Agatha paused, making sure they were all paying attention. "Everything Naveen told us today corresponds with the statement he gave to Deshpande," she said. "But the captain didn't check out his alibi. The boy at reception confirmed that Naveen Chandra never left his room on the night of the theft."

Dash choked on his jasmine rice. "What?" he coughed. "Didn't you say yourself that he could have just climbed out his window?"

Agatha signaled her companions to follow her to the balcony railing. "Look down," she said, pointing at the undisturbed muddy soil under Naveen Chandra's window. "No footprints. And even if he let himself down with a rope—well, you can see for yourselves." The walls of the hotel were surrounded by a dense thicket of mangroves, bamboo canes, and spiny plants.

"He couldn't have gone that way, not even with a machete," Uncle Rudyard commented wryly. "He'd be covered with scratches."

Agatha turned to her cousin. "Did you notice any cuts or bandages on Naveen Chandra today?" she asked.

"Hmm, let me think," Dash ruminated. "Nope. Not a scratch."

"So his alibi stands, and Captain Deshpande has got the wrong man," Agatha concluded.

Everybody agreed.

Only Dash, who'd been hoping to fly back to school with an easy A, seemed a bit disappointed.

As darkness fell, the five companions set out to tell Captain Deshpande about his mistake.

"Naveen Chandra's arrest could actually work in our favor," mused Agatha, tapping her nose with her finger. "The real culprit will be feeling secure now, so he'll be more likely to let something slip."

"Good point," agreed Dash. Rudyard nodded.

"How do you plan to proceed, Miss?" asked Chandler.

"The Spanish tourists and Brahman Sangali are the only ones left on our list of suspects," said Dash. "Should we question them now?"

"One step at a time." Agatha smiled.

She pulled the folder of statements from her purse and showed Dash the names of the two Spaniards. "Could you please check their criminal records on your EyeNet?"

Dash nodded. "I'm on it."

He powered up his gadget, instantly accessing Eye International's criminal archive.

Looking over his shoulder, Uncle Rudyard watched him scroll down the long list. "You wouldn't be able to get me one of those thingamajiggers, would you?" he whispered. "Be handy for tracking down poachers!"

Dash's eyes were fixed on the fast-moving

screen, and he didn't reply. Then he exclaimed, "Incredible! Got 'em!"

"Let's hear it," said Agatha. "What did you find?"

Dash began rattling off his discoveries. "They've done heists all over the world! Listen to this: a solid-glass model of the Eiffel Tower in Paris, a miniature Colosseum from Rome, a Mickey Mouse puppet from Disneyland. It goes on and on!"

Agatha burst out laughing. The others looked at her, stunned.

"What's so funny?" hissed Dash, his pride wounded. "They're international criminals!"

Chandler and Uncle Rudyard looked at Agatha, waiting.

"Puppets and souvenirs aren't the usual loot for professional thieves," she explained. "I just flipped through one of my memory drawers and pictured one of Mom's medical texts. I was

skimming through it a couple of months ago . . ." She paused for a moment, closing her eyes in concentration. When she reopened them, she asked in a whisper, "Have you ever heard of kleptomania?"

Chandler frowned. "Give us a hint," said Dash.

"It's an uncontrollable urge to steal objects that have little value, just for the pleasure of doing it," Agatha explained as Uncle Rudyard scanned the list of thefts on the EyeNet.

"This is a list of trinkets!" he snorted. "It's all worthless junk!"

"Since the Bengal Pearl is invaluable," Chandler concluded, "it seems obvious they didn't steal it."

"Excellent deduction!" Agatha congratulated him.

Dash slumped back into his seat, sighing deeply.

Agatha passed Watson a tidbit of tandoori chicken. "Don't worry, Dash," she consoled him. "Deshpande's list still has one name on it: Brahman Sangali. Do you know him, Uncle?"

Rudyard Mistery shook his head. "Never met the man."

"All right, let's go have a chat with him," proposed the girl. She picked up her purse and headed downstairs. Watson trotted behind her.

The others quickly followed, switching on their flashlights as they left the Tiger Hotel.

It was just past 7:30, but there were few lights in the village. The people of Chotoka rose with the sun and had already retired to their homes to sleep. There wasn't a living soul on the main street as Agatha and her companions made their way toward the temple. The road became steeper and narrower the farther they went into the jungle. Dash tried very hard not to think about scorpions, snakes, leopards, and tigers.

After a short while, they heard voices. Snapping off their flashlights, they walked forward cautiously until they reached the edge of a clearing where a group of faithful devotees sang sacred chants by the glow of small fires.

The air was thick with the musky scent of incense. Through the spiraling smoke, Agatha caught sight of the ancient sanctuary. Her mouth fell open.

It was a square stone tower, some forty feet tall, surrounded by narrow stone steps. Every level was decorated with frescoes and stone carvings dedicated to the goddess Kali. In the flickering firelight, it gave off a spooky, menacing air.

"Look, there's a guard at the temple door," whispered Dash. "Captain Deshpande still has it under surveillance."

"That's strange," Chandler said. "Since he already thinks he's got the culprit."

"Maybe he's waiting until Amitav Chandra

is found, too," suggested Uncle Rudyard in his booming voice.

The groups of kneeling devotees suddenly realized they weren't alone and stopped chanting their sacred litany.

One of them stood up abruptly, advancing in large strides, his finger to his lips. He wore a black tunic that left his sinewy arms bare, and a full white beard framed his face.

In spite of his priestly robes, he had a sinister presence.

Agatha decided to make the first move. "Good evening, Brahman Sangali," she whispered, clasping her hands and bowing.

He paused for a moment, then signaled to the devotees to resume their chanting. Then he ushered the foreigners behind a large tree. "Have we met before, Miss?" he asked in a low voice.

The girl followed her instincts. "Amitav Chandra told me about your differences of

opinion," she lied. "You two didn't agree on much, did you?"

Brahman Sangali looked very uncomfortable. "We had different duties," he mumbled. "He was the temple's custodian, and I oversee the sacred rituals. It's normal for minor disagreements to come up from time to time."

Dash understood Agatha's plan. She was putting the priest under pressure so that he would tell them as much as possible.

"Did you plot to steal the Pearl of Bengal?" she asked bluntly. "Maybe with the help of your followers?"

Uncle Rudyard and Chandler folded their arms, waiting for his reply.

"Never!" the Brahman exclaimed indignantly. "Only a foreigner could think such a thing! Do you know what grave misfortunes will befall our village if the pearl is not recovered? We are praying night and day that it be returned to our goddess. Kali is the Mother of the World for us Hindus, the most powerful deity of all. She is the only one who can save us from disasters, from war, and from the earth's sicknesses. We would not dare to offend her and encourage her wrath!" His voice shook with terror.

After this heartfelt outpouring, Agatha was certain Sangali was telling the truth. His words matched what she had read about Kali and the Hindu religion. She apologized to the Brahman for questioning him so rudely, explaining that they, too, were doing their best to recover the priceless pearl.

Still shaken, the priest accepted her apology, and added, "Would you care to join in our chanting?"

"As you say, we are foreigners," said Agatha tactfully. Then a strange idea struck her. "Brahman, have any new pilgrims arrived in the last few weeks?"

Sangali reflected. "Three, perhaps four," he replied vaguely.

"Could you point them out to me, please?"

They turned back to the clearing in front of the temple.

The priest hesitated. "It is not easy to see who is who in the dark," he admitted. "And well, you know, pilgrims come and go. It's easy to mistake one for another."

The girl observed the kneeling devotees, swaying in front of their flickering fires. For a split second, one of the men seemed familiar, but the sensation vanished immediately.

The small group walked back toward the Tiger Hotel. Uncle Rudyard said good night at the gate, continuing on to the dock where the raft to his seaplane was moored.

Before she slipped under the sheets, Agatha reviewed Deshpande's list of suspects with Dash and Chandler. They had eliminated every last one from suspicion. So who was the thief?

They fell asleep with no answer in sight.

But they had completely forgotten the one hotel guest who remained in the garden, watching the light in their bedroom click off: the gentleman with the pince-nez glasses who'd been reading the newspaper that afternoon.

The Statue of Kali

*L*ittle Parama darted back and forth, balancing breakfast trays like a professional acrobat. When she brought the pot of chai tea to their table, Agatha gave her a generous tip. Then she raised her face to the morning sun, inhaling the cinnamon scent of the sweet, frothy drink.

At 7:30 in the morning, the village of Chotoka was peaceful. The fishermen had left at dawn, and the other villagers quietly went about their business, unhurried and smiling.

It was like a little corner of paradise.

Without warning, the hotel's bell began

ringing wildly. Parama went to the gate and returned with Uncle Rudyard.

Rudyard Mistery was red-faced from running. "Have you heard the news?" he gasped.

"What?" asked Dash with his mouth full of stuffed dosa pancakes.

Uncle Rudyard gestured toward the river. "One of the forest guards just came to order me to move my seaplane away from the dock," he panted, bending to catch his breath. "And do you know why?"

"No," the three Londoners replied in chorus.

"Captain Deshpande has sent for the police from Kolkata," he continued. "A boat will arrive by midday to pick up Naveen Chandra!"

"You're joking!" said Agatha. The teacup shook in her hand. But one look at Rudyard's face told her he was all too serious. "There's no time to lose. We have to help Naveen!" she declared.

"Why don't we tell Deshpande his alibi's

valid?" asked Dash. "And that we can prove it!"

"It's not going to work, cousin. The captain's convinced himself that Naveen is guilty. All he's waiting for is his confession!"

Dash ran his hand through his hair. "We've only got four hours!" he cried, on the verge of panic. "What can we possibly do in such a short time?"

Chandler raised an eyebrow. "Find the real culprit?" he asked drily.

"Well, duh! But we're groping around in the dark!" Dash moaned.

Agatha rushed to the reception desk and came back with a map of the Sundarbans National Park. She spread it on the table and studied it for several minutes.

Meanwhile Dash paced in circles, repeating, "We don't have a clue! Literally! How can we catch a thief with no evidence?"

Agatha stared at her cousin, then back at the

map. Intuition lit up her eyes. "Dash, you're a genius!" she chortled.

He froze in his tracks. "I'm a genius?" he asked in a strangled voice. "I'm the worst detective in history!"

"No, you're a genius!" Agatha said. "We've been following Deshpande's list instead of conducting a real investigation based on evidence and clues. We need to fix that immediately!"

"But the Temple of Kali is under surveillance," Dash said. "How will we get inside it?"

"I have an idea," whispered Agatha, pulling them closer and pointing at a spot on the map. She quickly explained her plan while the others nodded with growing enthusiasm. Then she asked, "How long will it take, Uncle Rudyard?"

"Ten minutes by plane to get there, an hour and a half to return overland."

Agatha checked her watch. "Perfect! All right

then, let's meet at the Temple of Kali at ten on the dot!"

Uncle Rudyard handed her one of his many cameras, equipped with a zoom lens. Then he and Chandler sped off to their secret destination.

As soon as the two men disappeared, Dash voiced his doubts. "This is our last hope. Are you sure it'll work?"

"Of course!" exclaimed Agatha.

"So what do we do now?"

"We relax. And I'm going to finish my chai while we wait," she said with a smile.

The minutes passed slowly, like sand trickling through an hourglass. Dash paced around the garden, every so often casting an eye at the street. Agatha sat at the table, stroking Watson and jotting down notes in her notebook. No more words were exchanged till she picked up her purse and calmly announced, "Time to go."

Putting on a brave front, Dash strode through

the village with confidence. But as soon as they were surrounded by jungle, he slowed down, flinching at shrieking monkeys and rustling leaves. Just before they reached the temple, he stopped short and turned to face Agatha. "Is this close enough?" he asked nervously.

"These tree ferns offer excellent cover." His cousin nodded. Crouching behind a bush, she took out Rudyard's camera, using its long lens as a telescope like the housebound photographer in *Rear Window*. She zoomed from the small group of pilgrims at prayer and the guard at the door. It was amazing how close they appeared.

Cautiously Dash crouched beside her.

"What time is it?" Agatha asked, and he glanced at his EyeNet.

"Five to ten. Think they'll get here on time?"

"Calm down, Dash. It will all go according to plan!"

Just at that moment, a bloodcurdling roar

echoed through the jungle. The devotees stopped chanting, and the guard swiveled, pulling a pistol out of his belt.

Another roar sounded, much closer this time.

The pilgrims bunched together, asking one another what was happening. Suddenly a tiger appeared on the steps of the temple. Everyone screamed in terror.

It was a mighty, lithe, majestic beast.

The tiger stepped forward hungrily.

When it roared for the third time, the pilgrims fled toward the village, practically flying past the cousins' hiding place. The guard scrambled after them, too scared to shoot.

Watson emerged from the bushes, bravely stepping forward to meet the wild beast.

The Siberian cat and the Bengal tiger sniffed each other with curiosity. Then Uncle Rudyard strode out of the jungle, grinning from ear to ear. "Good girl, Maya, well done!" he said to the tiger,

giving her a gentle pat on the neck. Agatha and Chandler joined him in praising the tiger, while Dash kept a safe distance.

"Did your colleagues at the tiger reserve give you any trouble about this?" asked Agatha.

Uncle Rudyard winked. "I just said I was taking my girl for a little walk," he chuckled. "And now it's time to go back home, right, Maya?"

He pulled out a collar and leash, but the tiger thought it was a game and bounded away, disappearing into the lush vegetation. "She's feeling frisky. I'd better go get her, kids," their uncle said. "Go on into the temple without me!"

He didn't need to tell them twice.

The lock was still broken, and Chandler nudged the door open with his flashlight. They slipped inside, pulling the door shut in case someone came back and noticed. It was pitch-black and the thick, dusty air smelled of incense.

The circular beam of the flashlight skimmed over the walls, illuminating colorful tapestries, inlaid wooden carvings, bronze vases filled with scented oils, and countless other offerings.

The atmosphere inside the temple was rich and mysterious.

The roaming flashlight beam suddenly fell on the gigantic statue of Kali behind the altar.

"Arrrgh!" yelled Dash. "What kind of monster is that?!"

He instinctively jumped behind Agatha, who stared at the statue in wonder.

It was easily twelve feet tall. The goddess

was depicted as a fearsome woman warrior with four arms, and her tongue was sticking out in a hideous grimace. Her skin was black, her robes sheathed with a layer of gold. Three severed heads hung from her belt, and a garland of miniature skulls fell across her chest.

"Don't be fooled by her looks," whispered Agatha. "Kali the Black is a goddess of war, but that's only one of her many aspects. She protects humankind from demons." She cast a bright smile at her cousin. "And she's very vengeful with people who act like cowards."

Dash pulled himself together. "Quick! Look for clues!"

He and Chandler began scouring the room while Agatha took her flashlight and pointed it up at the statue's four hands. "If memory serves me correctly, Kali wields a sword, a shield, a cup, and a snare," she said aloud to herself.

The cup was missing.

Kali's right hand, held highest in the air, was empty.

"The Bengal Pearl was taken from there," she told her companions. "Can someone please help me up?"

"Right away, Miss!" replied Chandler.

The butler laced his fingers together and boosted her up. Agatha tried to steady herself, touching Kali's face. "If I could just reach that top hand," she said feverishly. "But it's too far away!"

"How could they have taken the pearl from way up there?" asked Dash.

Agatha suddenly froze. She was touching the tip of Kali's nose, her thinking position.

"What's wrong, Miss?" asked Chandler.

The girl didn't reply. Her mind was working overtime.

"What's going on?" asked Dash. "Did you find a clue?"

Agatha muttered along with her racing thoughts.

"Twelve feet high . . . No room for a ladder . . . No way to climb up the statue . . ." Then she exclaimed, "Oh, of course!"

"Of course what?"

"The thief used some sort of a tool to push the cup out of her hand . . . something long!" She picked up the camera, zooming in on Kali's hand. There were a few green wood shavings in the statue's palm. "I've got it!" she cried joyfully. "I know who committed the theft!"

Just then, the door swung open and someone advanced on them.

Agatha's first thought was that it must be Uncle Rudyard, but one glance at the man's swirling robes told her it wasn't him.

The pilgrim stepped forward. Pointing his pistol right at them, he pulled the hood from his head.

His face was familiar. In fact, it was all too familiar.

The face of an actor.

"Naveen Chandra?!" they all yelled in amazement.

The Final Verdict

*A*gatha's mind reeled. So that was the face she thought she'd recognized among the devotees praying at the temple last night!

Flowing black hair, strong chin, elegant bearing . . . it was definitely Naveen Chandra!

But wasn't he locked up in jail?

Steadying herself against Kali's hand, Agatha carefully climbed down to join Chandler and Dash, who were standing stock-still with their hands raised in the air. "Naveen?" she said softly. "Put down the gun. We know you didn't steal it."

The man gestured with his gun, signaling that

they should all exit the temple. He did not say a word, but glared at them with menacing rage.

Dash obeyed, edging along the wall of the dark room.

In the narrow space, Chandler bumped into a brass vase, spilling essential oil over the floor. Just as Agatha started to follow him out, the temple door was flung open again.

"I collared that smart-aleck Maya!" said Uncle Rudyard as he stepped inside.

The assailant spun around, pointing the gun at him.

As he did, Chandler leaped at him as if he were back in the boxing ring. "Face me, you scoundrel!" he shouted. "I never hit someone from behind!"

The man swiveled in terror, stepping into a knockout right hook. It was just a single punch to the jaw, but with all the power and skill of an experienced heavyweight boxer. The poor man

slumped to the ground like a sack of rice.

The room echoed with cheers.

"That's quite a punch, big man!" exclaimed Uncle Rudyard. "Why did you ever retire from the ring?"

Dash was grinning from ear to ear.

Agatha knelt to check on their unconscious assailant. She pulled up one eyelid. "Look here," she breathed. "Take a good look at his eyes!"

They weren't Naveen's striking peacock blue, but plain brown.

"He's the spitting image of Naveen Chandra in all other ways. Maybe he was his body double in his movies," she reflected. Touching her nose, she added, "And I think I know why he came to the village disguised as a pilgrim."

The others looked blank. Agatha started to fill them in, but stopped short as she noticed the time. "It's already eleven thirty. We have to get to the dock before the police come for Naveen!"

Chandler threw the unconscious man over one shoulder, and they hurried away.

Twenty minutes later, an unusual group arrived at the village steps: two burly men, one lugging an unconscious pilgrim; two English children; a white Persian cat; and a Bengal tiger on a leash.

Captain Deshpande was chatting with a police officer while a handcuffed Naveen Chandra was being led up the gangplank onto the police boat.

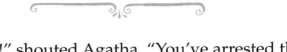

"Stop!" shouted Agatha. "You've arrested the wrong man!"

They all turned to stare at the new arrivals. The policeman watched as Chandler lifted the pilgrim's face. The resemblance to Naveen was unmistakable. Turning to Captain Deshpande, he asked, "What's going on? Is this some kind of joke?"

"It's nonsense!" the captain replied in an arrogant tone. "Forget these young pests! They think they're some kind of detectives. They just want to look good for their bosses!"

"Oh, we will look good, Captain!" Agatha smiled, slowly descending the stairs. "Especially after this nice police officer arrests the man who's actually responsible for kidnapping Amitav Chandra and stealing the Pearl of Bengal!"

Deshpande exploded with fury. "Are you crazy? Who's going to believe a word you kids say?" he shouted. "This is the Kolkata police!

You're obstructing an investigation!"

The officer touched his arm. "Something's not right here, Captain," he said. "If you don't mind, I'd like to hear from these two young detectives."

On the riverbank, surrounded by policemen and forest guards, Agatha and Dash began telling their story.

"Our agency received a call from Amitav Chandra, the temple custodian," said Dash, clicking open an audio file on his EyeNet.

The officer listened to the recording with a skeptical expression.

"At first, we thought Mr. Chandra was asking his friend Deshpande for help, but listen carefully to the last part." He pressed the rewind button.

"If anything happens to me, tell my dear friend . . . KSSHHH KSSSHHH . . . Deshpande! . . . BEEP-BEEP-BEEP-BEEP . . .

The name "Deshpande" sounded as if it was uttered in shock, as though Mr. Chandra had

been caught by surprise by the captain himself.

"This means nothing," the captain interrupted abruptly. "We have several witnesses who saw his son Naveen break into his house!"

"Of course you do," said Agatha calmly. "Only it wasn't Naveen, but his body double, who's been hiding among the pilgrims all this time! He was the person the neighbors spotted that night, and that's how you managed to pin the theft on Naveen. Am I right?"

"That's a despicable charge," snarled Deshpande. "Arrest these children!"

"Wait just a second, Captain," the officer interrupted drily. "I want to hear how this story turns out. Go on, kids."

Agatha took a deep breath. "The body double and Captain Deshpande led Amitav Chandra to the temple at gunpoint, trying to force him to open the door with the key combination that only he knew," she explained. "When he wouldn't,

they broke the lock. Once they were inside, they couldn't figure out how to get the Pearl of Bengal down from the statue's hand. Captain Deshpande started pushing the cup with his cane and finally caused it to fall."

She looked at the captain, who leaned crookedly on his cane. "We found chips of bamboo in Kali's hand, Captain," she added, unfolding her palm to display them. "I'm sure the police will be able to match them."

"And then?" the officer urged.

"Then Deshpande hid the pearl and Mr. Chandra in a safe place and calmly began his investigation," said Agatha, beaming. "All he needed to do was find enough witnesses to point the finger at Mr. Chandra's son. But we spoiled his plans!"

"How so, Miss?"

"When we arrived, he gave us a list of fake suspects as a ploy to keep us busy. But he forbade

us to see Chandra's home or the Temple of Kali, putting both under guard."

She paused, then added indignantly, "He even organized a search party on the river to show us how much he cared about his missing friend, when all he was doing was finding a fisherman who could support his lies!"

"I'm with you so far, Miss," the officer said. "But tell me, where is Mr. Chandra hidden? Where is the Pearl of Bengal?"

Agatha winked. "If I were a policeman and not some 'young pest,'" she said calmly, "I would start by inspecting the captain's house. You might even find some costumes used by his accomplice, Naveen Chandra's body double."

At that moment, Deshpande tried to bolt, lurching toward the steps. But his path was blocked by Chandler, Uncle Rudyard—and a hungry Bengal tiger.

He dropped to his knees in surrender. "I just

wanted to retire in comfort," he sobbed, slumping his shoulders. "As soon as the excitement died down, I would have freed my friend Amitav. I didn't murder anyone!"

The officer nodded to his colleagues on board the police boat. They took the handcuffs off Naveen Chandra, arresting Captain Deshpande and his accomplice instead. "That's some fancy detective work, kids," he said, turning to Dash and Agatha. "What is your agency called?"

"I'm not at liberty to say, sir!" exclaimed Dash, hugging Agatha happily. "But I'm called Agent DM14!"

The two cousins realized that the whole village had gathered around the steps, bursting into applause when the mystery was solved.

"We did it!" Dash repeated, heading into the crowd to embrace Uncle Rudyard. But instead, he bumped into an elderly gentleman holding up the *London Times*.

He was wearing a linen suit and pince-nez glasses.

"Wh-who are you?" Dash stammered.

The gentleman lowered the newspaper, looking him right in the eye. "Hello, Agent DM14," he said. "I am your fieldwork observer. I wanted to congratulate you in person. Eye

International wants you to know that you did an excellent job. You passed the test with flying colors, Agent." This said, he disappeared into the crowd without so much as a ripple.

Dash stood frozen, his eyes wide, until Agatha shook him. "What's up, cousin? You look a bit dazed. Too much excitement?" she asked cheerfully.

His cousin was right, as always. Dash was filled to the brim with excitement and a joy beyond words.

Mystery Solved...

The police found Amitav Chandra bound and gagged inside a large closet in Deshpande's house. The Bengal Pearl was hidden inside the toe of an embroidered boot. Brahman Sangali was notified immediately, and he gathered the whole village to take the sacred pearl back to the Temple of Kali in a grand procession.

Amitav Chandra and his son, Naveen, also joined the colorful, festive parade, having finally reconciled.

Right behind them were Agatha and her companions.

"Why don't you come back to Mumbai

with me?" Naveen Chandra asked the kids. "I could give you both walk-on roles in my next blockbuster. You'd have a blast! Mumbai is a wonderful city, and there's nothing more fun than the set of a Bollywood movie."

Dash was about to say yes when Agatha reminded him of their promise. "I'm sorry, Naveen, but we're going straight to New Delhi," she said, loosening the garland of marigolds around her neck, a gift from the people of Chotoka. "We're going to surprise my parents!"

Naveen seemed quite moved. Evidently the events of the past few days had made him rethink things. "Never forget how important your parents are, kids," he said solemnly. "And listen to their advice sometimes. Every so often, they're right!"

Dash and Agatha nodded and laughed.

Behind them, Uncle Rudyard was asking Chandler's advice about boxing, miming

punches in the air. "Should I hold my shoulder like this? Or like this?" he asked over and over. "Like this, right?"

The butler nodded in silence for the hundredth time. He couldn't take it anymore; Rudyard had been grilling him on his best punches all day.

As the sun went down over the river, the festival turned into a banquet, with course after course of delicious food. Everyone happily stuffed themselves with local delicacies.

Without even pausing to lick his whiskers,

Watson devoured a plate of fish, fresh from the Ganges.

Uncle Rudyard was full and almost asleep on his feet. He had made quite a long trek through the jungle to bring Maya back to the tiger reserve. Then he'd flown back in his seaplane.

"You can be the lead pilot this time, slugger!" he told Chandler, seating him at the controls. "Do you know how to take off from on the water?"

Dash changed his mind about the earlier flight. This was the worst takeoff of his life.

The Canadair shaved the tops of the trees like an incompetent barber for the first mile or two, then drifted between the brilliant stars toward New Delhi.

The children awoke at dawn when Watson began yowling for breakfast.

"Have we been flying all night?" Agatha asked, stunned by the pink glow of sunrise.

Uncle Rudyard turned around in the cockpit, as lively as ever. "I dozed off for a bit, and the big man got lost," he shouted. "We're just passing over the Himalayas!" he laughed. "Say hello to Mount Everest!" Then he started to sing at the top of his lungs, oblivious to Chandler, who'd fallen asleep in the passenger seat.

They touched down in New Delhi at eight in the morning.

"Hello, Mom?" said Agatha into the EyeNet's speakerphone.

"Why, Agatha darling! How are you?" replied Rebecca Mistery.

"I'm great! Listen, I have a surprise for you and Dad."

"Oh good, what?"

"I'm here in New Delhi, Mom!" Agatha told her. "With Dash, Watson, and Chandler. And Uncle Rudyard, too!"

This was greeted by sounds of distressed rumbling on the other end of the phone. Dash moved closer to listen.

"What's the matter, Mom? Is there a problem?" asked Agatha.

"Oh, it's nothing, dear . . . Just a bull elephant having a bit of a tantrum!"

"An elephant?" Dash squawked.

"We have a free day today," Mrs. Mistery continued. "So we thought we'd take a day trip to the Taj Mahal on elephant back! Your father is doing a wonderful job with the steering . . ."

Agatha laughed while Dash covered his face in despair.

"Would you like to join us?" her mother asked in a bubbly voice.

"No, say no!" whispered Dash frantically. "Right now, all I want is a hotel with a swimming pool, a cold drink, and some time to chill out!"

"We'd love to join you!" Agatha replied. "I can't wait to see the Taj Mahal!"

Dash slumped back, clutching his head. There was no such thing as time to chill out when your last name was Mistery!